A Kiss in My Pocket

Karen Paquette

Balboa Press books may be ordered through booksellers or by contacting:

Balboa Press
A Division of Hay House
1663 Liberty Drive
Bloomington, IN 47403
www.balboapress.com
1-(877) 407-4847

ISBN: 978-1-4525-8636-6 (sc)
ISBN: 978-1-4525-8637-3 (e)

Library of Congress Control Number: 2013922378

Printed in the United States of America.

Balboa Press rev. date: 01/28/2014

BALBOA
PRESS
A DIVISION OF HAY HOUSE

With Love to Our Amazing Grandchildren
Julie, Jenna, Natalie
Minda, Soleil and Jonah
Six of Life's Greatest Blessings!

I love visiting Grandma. When it's
time to leave Grandma puts a kiss
in my pocket. Grandma's kiss makes
me smile and makes my heart sing.

Mom wants me to wear a dress today. No! I have to wear my overalls with Grandma's kiss in the pocket.

After I get dressed I look in my pocket to make sure Grandma's kiss is still there. Grandma says the kiss is there even if I can't see it.

At the playground, I fall and scrape my knee. It really hurts! Mom puts a pink bandage on my knee which makes me feel a tiny bit better.

Then I remember Grandma's kiss. I take Grandma's kiss out of my pocket and put it on my knee. Now I feel much better.

Sometimes my baby brother cries and cries. Mom doesn't know what to do.

I take Grandma's kiss out of my pocket
and give the kiss to my baby brother.
I whisper to him, "It's a kiss from
Grandma." Grandma's kiss makes him
happy and he smiles and laughs at me.

At lunch we have green peas. Yuck! I don't like green peas. Mom says, "Eat three peas because you are three."

I put the peas in my pocket with my kiss. Grandma's kiss will make the peas taste better.

We walk to the library. It's my
favourite place. I love sitting
in the Blue Bear chair to read.

Someone is sitting in the Blue Bear chair. I have to wait my turn and it makes me sad. Soon it's time to go and I have not had my turn to sit in the Blue Bear chair.

I reach in my pocket for Grandma's
kiss and instead I get green
pea mush on my library book.

Mom and the Librarian are upset with me.
Mom cleans the book and my hand with a
tissue and throws the tissue in the trash.

"Mom, what about Grandma's kiss?"

"Naptime," Mom declares
and home we go.

Mom gives me my favorite blanket, my alligator flashlight, my floppy bunny and my red ladybug pillow. What I really want is Grandma's kiss. I reach into my pocket to see if it might be there.

I use my alligator flashlight just
to make sure. Then I remember
that Grandma says the kiss is
there even if I cannot see it.

Laundry day. Mom says we have to wash my overalls. We can't wash Grandma's kiss. I take the kiss out of my pocket but where can I put it?

Mom hands me a skirt with a
butterfly pocket. No, that won't
work. The kiss will fall out.

Mom finds red pants with pockets everywhere. She shows me a special pocket by the knee with a secret pocket inside. I carefully put Grandma's kiss in the secret pocket to keep it safe.

Tomorrow we are going to Grandma's house again! I am excited to see my Grandma and show her my secret pocket.

Grandma thinks the secret pocket
is the perfect place for kisses.
When it's time to leave Grandma
puts another kiss in my pocket.